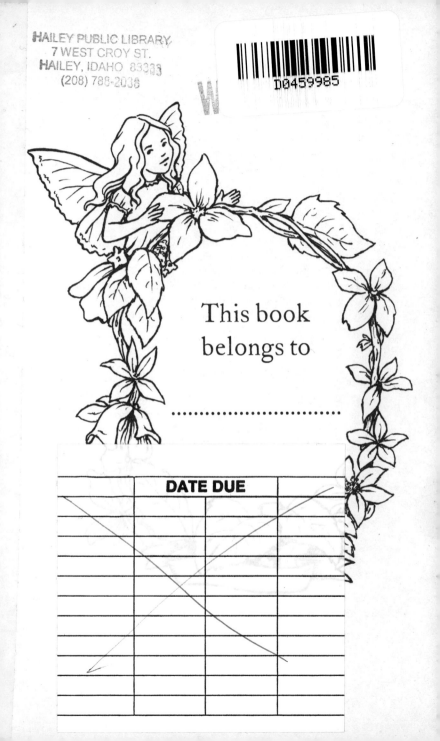

D0459985

This book
belongs to

....

DATE DUE

FREDERICK WARNE

Published by the Penguin Group
Penguin Books Ltd, 80 Strand, London WC2R 0RL, England
Penguin Young Readers Group, 345 Hudson Street,
New York, New York 10014, U.S.A.
Penguin Books Australia Ltd, 250 Camberwell Road, Camberwell,
Victoria 3124, Australia
Canada, India, New Zealand, South Africa

1 3 5 7 9 10 8 6 4 2

ISBN: 978 07232 5972 5

Printed in Great Britain

Merry Fairy
Holidays

Welcome to the Flower Fairies' Garden!

Where are the fairies?
Where can we find them?
We've seen the fairy-rings
They leave behind them!

Is it a secret
No one is telling?
Why, in your garden
Surely they're dwelling!

No need for journeying,
Seeking afar:
Where there are flowers,
There fairies are!

Contents

Holly's Christmas Riddle

By Pippa Le Quesne

Contents

Chapter One
Christmas is Coming

"O, I am green in Winter-time,
When other trees are brown;
Of all the trees (So saith the rhyme)
The holly bears the crown . . ."

Holly bellowed the words of his song as he
skipped and hopped through the Flower
Fairies' Garden. Nothing could spoil his
high spirits today. Christmas—his favorite
time of year—was just around the corner.

The air was filled with the scent of cinnamon and the sound of jingling bells and the twinkle of fairy lights. It was *so* festive!

"Hey!" cried Yew. The Flower Fairy was perched on a high branch of his tree, chewing the end of a quill. "Keep the noise down! I'm trying to write a letter to Santa Claus."

"Sorry!" Holly whispered loudly. He shaded his eyes against the low winter sun and peered upwards. "Why not ask for some earplugs?" he teased. "Then you won't be deafened by my singing!" He flapped his spiky white wings and fluttered away, with the merry sound of Yew's giggles fading behind him.

"Yoohoo!" he called, to anyone who would listen. "It's nearly Christmas!"

"We know!" replied Sweet Pea and her younger sister. They were carefully wrapping presents in dried petals and tying them with blades of grass. "How's the Fairy Grotto?"

"Ooops!" Holly froze mid-hop. He'd been so busy touring the garden that he'd completely forgotten about the super-important job he had to do.

Every December, Holly was responsible for decking out the Fairy Grotto—a small clearing that nestled at the foot of his tree. This was where the garden Flower Fairies flocked on Christmas Eve to sing carols, share tasty treats and spend a few enchanting hours before the huge excitement of Christmas Day itself. Perhaps the best

moment of all was when the Flower Fairies' letters were sent on their way to Santa Claus. Fairies came from far and wide to watch this truly magical event.

"See you later!" cried Holly, neatly pirouetting on one emerald-green shoe and scurrying back the way he'd come. "Holly . . . ivy . . . and mistletoe," he muttered as he ran. "And oodles and oodles of fairy dust. Now, where will I find some candles . . ?"

The Lords-and-Ladies fairy chuckled as Holly whizzed past. "Did he forget?" he asked Spindle Berry.

The little fairy shook with laughter. "Yes," she said. "Again. Every year he forgets and rushes around like a supersonic bumblebee, yet every year the Fairy Grotto looks amazing. There's really no need for him to be panicking."

But Holly wasn't so sure. With less than

two days to go, he really had left it until the
last minute this year. Would the Fairy Grotto
really be ready by Christmas Eve?

By the time he reached his magnificent tree,
Holly was in quite a state. His cheeks were
flushed brighter than the red berries strung

around his waist and decorating his hood
and shoes, and his matching red stockings
were terribly wrinkled. But he didn't have
any intention of wasting time by looking at
his reflection in the stream and straightening
himself out. He had far more urgent things
to do!

Using a small piece of flint, he gently
cut sprigs of holly from his glorious tree,
whispering soothing words as he did so. He
deliberately chose branches that were heavily
laden with clusters of bright red berries.
These would look splendid dotted around
the Fairy Grotto. He was soon whistling

happily, his panic totally forgotten.

Even though the glossy, dark green leaves were edged with sharp points, Holly never felt the slightest prickle. It was the same with Rose and her thorns, he knew. Whether it was their plants' way of saying thank you for looking after them so well or because they had extra-thick skin, neither fairy knew. They just never had occasion to squeal, "*Ouch!*"

By nightfall, Holly was dying for an acorn of elderberry juice and a slab of Poppy's

delicious seed cake. And he wouldn't have said no to one of Mallow's fairy cheeses or a helping of Crab-apple's jelly either. He was a *very* hungry Flower Fairy. But he was very pleased too, because at the foot of the tree, there was an enormous, festive, green-and-red heap of holly. He fluttered to the ground and saw to his amazement that the results of his hard work reached higher than his head!

"My, you have been busy," said a soft voice.

Holly looked up to see a stem of fiery orange berries glowing in the dusky darkness. "Hello?" he said cautiously.

"It's me, silly!" said Lords-and-Ladies fairy, his orange outfit as bright as his berries. "I thought you might need something to brighten up your Fairy Grotto, so I've brought you one of my berry candles. Where would you like it?"

Holly grinned. "Over here, please," he

said, pointing to the edge of the clearing. "Thank you so much—that'll brighten things up nicely!"

"No problem," said the obliging Flower Fairy, adding, "Plenty more where that came from. Listen, I've got a couple of spare hours. Is there anything I can do to help?"

Nearly speechless with delight, Holly grabbed his friend's hand and pumped it up and down. "Oh, that would be great!" he gasped. "Marvellous ... simply marvellous." And within minutes, Lords-and-Ladies was busily carrying bundles of twigs to and fro, while Holly leapt about like an excited flea, decorating the edge of the clearing with arches of twisted holly.

A familiar song suddenly reached their ears, carried on a wintry gust of wind. Holly looked up in surprise, but his smiles soon turned downwards. It was *his* tune—but they *weren't* his words.

"O, I'm horrid and spiky in Winter-time,
When others are so bare;
Of all fairies (So saith the rhyme)
It's Holly you must beware ..."

"W-w-what?" stuttered Holly. He looked at Lords-and-Ladies, as if hoping for an explanation, but the other Flower Fairy seemed just as shocked as he. Holly's lip wobbled dangerously, but he managed— just—to hold back the tears. "Who would make up such horrid words?" he wailed.

Chapter Two
Bad Flower Fairies

By the next morning, the story had spread to the very edges of Flower Fairyland. No one could quite believe that someone would tamper with the precious words of a fairy's song, never mind sing them out loud. The fact that it was so close to Christmas just made things worse.

The kind-hearted Flower Fairies rallied round, comforting Holly with hugs galore

and treats aplenty, but nothing they did could cheer him up. "What's the point in decorating the Fairy Grotto now?" he said sadly. "My heart just isn't in it." Instead, he spent his time wandering about the garden, half-heartedly searching for clues to the identity of the mysterious singers, until . . .

"Stop the press!" squawked a big, black crow. "Listen!" He swooped into the Flower Fairy Garden around midday, crash-landing

on to a frozen puddle and skidding across its surface.

"What?" asked Holly glumly. He doubted that anything the ragged bird had to say would cheer him up. The crow was well known for being a dreadful gossip.

"News!" cried the crow. "You heard it here first! Come and hear the news!" Attracted by the noise, a large crowd of fairies gathered around. The bird scanned his audience,

delighted to be the centre of attention.

"Get on with it!" heckled Cornflower from the back.

"Well," began the crow. "It's like this . . . I heard from Red Campion, who was chatting with Ribwort Plantain, who'd overheard Horned Poppy, who just happened to be passing Chicory when . . ."

"Yes?" said the fairies, pushing forward eagerly.

". . . White Bindweed was gossiping with the Black Medick Fairies," the crow continued. "And *they* heard—"

"*What?*" shouted Yew. He flapped his beautiful green and red wings warningly and at last the bird decided to spill his secrets.

"It's all because of the Bad Flower Fairies," croaked the crow in a voice so low and mysterious that everyone had to lean forwards to make out the words.

"There's no such thing!" cried Holly. Flower Fairies were the loveliest, kindest, most thoughtful, helpful and well-mannered creatures ever.

The very idea that a fairy could be

anything but good was ridiculous. It was preposterous. Quite frankly, it was *wrong*.

"It's true, I tell you," protested the crow. "Red Campion told me so."

Yew slung a comforting arm around Holly's shoulders. "And what exactly did Red Campion say?" he asked the bird.

The crow flapped his wings importantly. "He said that the Bad Flower Fairies had come to spoil Christmas," he croaked.

Horror-struck, the crowd moved back a step. This was terrible news!

"Tell us more," said Yew quietly.

And so the crow did. Scraggle-wort and Hazel-bumpkin were to blame. These two creatures came from beyond the marsh—the wild area that lay outside the Flower Fairies' pretty garden. They spent their time being naughty and playing nasty tricks. They tied children's shoelaces together when they weren't looking. They turned milk sour. Sometimes, they even tore out the very last page of a storybook, so the reader would never find out what happened. But what made the Bad Flower Fairies so different to all the other Flower Fairies was the fact that they didn't enjoy Christmas. And, worse still, they wanted to make sure that no one else enjoyed it either.

"Why don't they like Christmas?" asked Holly.

"Because no one ever invites them," cawed

the crow. "They get so cross that they never receive an invitation to the Fairy Grotto that they've vowed to ruin Christmas for everyone."

"Ooooh . . ." chorused the fairies. They muttered among themselves anxiously.

Holly frowned. "But if we've never heard of Scraggle-wort and Hazel-bumpkin, how can we invite them to our parties? Besides, everyone's always welcome—with or without an invitation." Then he had another thought. "Do you think it could have been the Bad Flower Fairies that I overheard singing?" he asked.

"Sounds like it to me," replied Yew. Crossly, he

put his hands on his hips and whirled to face the stunned crowd. "Listen!" he called. "Can't you see that we're playing into their hands? The more miserable we are, the happier these Bad Flower Fairies will be, because they really *will* have ruined our Christmas celebrations."

"Good heavens, you're right!" cried Holly. "I've been moping around feeling sorry for myself, when all along I should have been ignoring the silly song and getting on with my decorations. Well, that's all over now!" He took a deep breath, leapt into the air and clicked his heels together. "Merry Christmas, everyone!"

There were whoops and cheers of approval from the crowd.

Suddenly, Holly remembered the crow, who appeared rather confused by events. "I suggest you fly back to Red Campion," he said brightly, "and tell him to tell Ribwort Plantain and Horned Poppy and Chicory and White Bindweed and the Black Medick Fairies and any other fairies you might meet on the marsh, that the Christmas Eve celebrations in the Fairy Grotto are going ahead as usual. We'll make sure that the Bad Flower Fairies don't spoil things!"

"Hurrah!" cried Cornflower from the back of the crowd. "The more Flower Fairies, the merrier!"

Chapter Three
Strange Happenings

But despite these brave words, there was more trouble in the Flower Fairies' Garden as Christmas Eve approached . . .

The glow-worms went on strike. They refused point blank to light up the Fairy Grotto, as they did every single year, on the grounds that they were being unfairly treated.

"*What?*" said Holly, goggle-eyed with disbelief.

"It's tiring, low-paid work," said the chief glow-worm, who was curled up on a low branch of the mulberry tree. "We want shorter working hours, longer holidays, regular breaks, overtime and paid sick leave."

"But it's the season of goodwill!" protested Holly.

"Don't care," the glow-worm answered back. "We know our rights. If our demands aren't met, you'll have to find another way of lighting your grotto." And he wriggled away grumpily.

This sort of behavior was totally unheard of in the Flower Fairies' Garden. The little creatures were usually so obliging. But Holly soon realized that even though he didn't know why the glow-worms were grumpy, it was important to cheer them up. After all, it was Christmas.

So the kind-hearted Flower Fairy took a selection of the juiciest mulberry leaves to the glow-worms. They, in turn, were so thrilled that they called off their strike at once, saying that they didn't know what had come over them.

It was all very strange.

Christmas was nearly here. And now,
everyone was so determined to make sure
that the Fairy Grotto was truly splendid that
Holly had no shortage of helpers. In a very
short time, the clearing was festooned with
glossy green holly leaves and luscious red
berries. Bunches of silvery-white mistletoe
hung above the grotto, linked by great
swags of greeny-white ivy.

Then the Bad Flower Fairies struck

again. In the few short moments that Holly left the grotto to write *his* letter to Santa Claus, berries were plucked from the holly twigs and scattered over the ground. It was as if the mysterious Scraggle-wort and Hazel-bumpkin had been bowling with them.

Holly put his hands on his hips and stared in utter bewilderment at the mess. None of this made any sense. The Bad Flower Fairies seemed to be everywhere. Yet no one ever saw them or even knew what they looked like. Now, they had managed to creep into the garden and perform all sorts of mischief without leaving a trace.

"Hmm," said a sharp voice. "I don't think much of your Christmas decorations."

"What?" said Holly.

There was no one there.

Holly looked left, right, left again, right again, then finally up to see an elf smirking

down at him. Dressed
entirely in green and wearing
a hat as pointy as his ears, the
cheeky creature was swinging to and fro
on a bendy twig and chuckling to himself.
Holly was outraged. Had the elf seen the
Bad Flower Fairies in action and done
nothing to stop them?

"Did you see them?" he demanded crossly.

"Who?" asked the elf. Then his grin grew
wider. "Oh, you mean Scraggy-wart and
Hazey-bump-bump? Yes, they were here..."
He leapt to the ground, landing right in front
of Holly.

"Scraggle-wort and Hazel-bumpkin?"
said Holly.

"Er, yes... that's right," said the elf. He
lowered his voice to a confidential whisper.
"They waited until you were gone and
then zoomed into the grotto like two mini

tornadoes. There were berries and leaves everywhere—it was total mayhem." The creature narrowed his eyes and leant closer. "If I were you, I'd just give up. The Bad Fairies always win."

"No!" cried Holly, springing away. "Not this time. I simply won't let them spoil Christmas!"

The elf shrugged. "It's up to you," he said with a sour laugh. And with a flutter of pointy wings, he was gone.

But now Holly was determined that the Fairy Grotto would be more magical than ever. And in the meantime, he would do a bit of fairy detective work to find the mischief-makers. In fact, a clever plan was forming in his head right now . . .

He began to tidy up the bright red berries, whistling 'Jingle Bells' as he worked. In the distance he heard singing:

"O, I am silly in Winter-time,
I like to play the clown;
Of all the fairies (So saith the rhyme)
It's Holly wears a gown . . ."

But this time, Holly just laughed.

Chapter Four
A Great Idea

"Wow!" said Spindle Berry. "It looks amazing..."

"Do you really think so?" asked Holly. "You're not just saying it to be nice?"

"No..." breathed the little fairy. She hugged her arms around her delicate dusky-pink frock and gently moved her pale orange wings to and fro, staring in awe at the mass

of green leaves and red berries. And was the floor really twinkling? *It was!* Somehow, Holly had carpeted the Fairy Grotto with a layer of sparkles.

Holly tapped his nose. "Fairy dust," he said. "I've been up all night making it."

Fairy dust took an exceedingly long time to make, but it was worth it. Each Flower Fairy made their very own dust from their

own plants. Many of the fairies used their flowers. Lavender, for example, gathered pollen, then ground it between two rough stones to make the tiny glittering particles. Holly used his bright red berries instead. These he picked and dried in the late-summer sun, waiting until they were touched by the very first frost of the winter. As soon as this happened, the dried, frozen berries

were packed into beechnut shells and ground to a fine powder with a blunt stick. Then, *ta-daaaa*, the fairy dust was ready—full of magic and packed with sparkles.

Holly looked all around and then decided to confide in Spindle Berry. "By the way, I've thought of a plan," he whispered.

"Ooooh," said Spindle Berry. Although she was one of the youngest Flower Fairies, she loved to hear her older friends' ideas. It was so much more exciting than hanging around with the babies.

"Well," said Holly. "I'm going to lay a trap. It'll be a trap so clever, so simple and so absolutely foolproof that the Bad Flower Fairies won't stand a chance." He grinned widely. "What do you think of *that*?"

Spindle Berry's eyebrows shot up. "What are you going to *do* to them?" she gasped, looking very worried.

Holly laughed loudly. "Oh, nothing too dreadful," he said. "You know, catch them. Then pelt them with rotten berries, make them do the washing-up after the party . . . That sort of thing."

Poor Spindle Berry looked like she might pass out from the shock. "But you *can't*!" she squealed. "That's not how Flower Fairies behave! What sort of example are you setting if—?" She stopped, suddenly realizing that Holly's shoulders were shaking with laughter. "You're kidding, aren't you?" she

said suspiciously.

"Of course I am," chuckled Holly. "I'm so sorry. I just couldn't resist!"

"So there's no grand plan?" asked Spindle Berry.

"Oh, there's a plan all right," replied Holly. "But my plan is to find Scraggle-wort and Hazel-bumpkin—and then help them to fall in love with Christmas too. Listen . . ." And he outlined his perfect plan.

First, Holly would let it be known that the Fairy Grotto was finished. Then, he would make sure that everyone knew he was going to spend that evening visiting friends on the far side of the garden. But, instead of seeing his friends, he would carefully position small bunches of holly leaves all around the Fairy Grotto—and then lie in wait for visitors.

"Ooooh," breathed Spindle Berry. "And then?"

"It'll be too dark to see, so I'll wait for the Bad Flower Fairies to step on the prickly leaves," said Holly. "At the first *ouch*, I'll have them! And, after I've told them a few festive tales, they'll be full to the brim with Christmas spirit. Before you know it, they'll be having a whale of a time."

"It's that easy?" asked Spindle Berry.

"Yep," said Holly. He'd never been convinced by the crow's story that these Flower Fairies didn't enjoy Christmas. They just needed a helping hand, that was all.

At dusk, Holly put the plan into action. He moved Lords-and-Ladies' candles behind his tree trunk, plunging the Fairy Grotto into darkness. Next, he carefully positioned holly leaves all around the edges of the clearing. (He made sure that they weren't too sharp. He was aiming for *ouch*, not *OUCH*.) And then he hid.

It was quiet, very quiet. Seconds passed, then minutes. An hour later, Holly was wondering if it had been such a good plan after all. He was sure that his nose was starting to glow with the cold.

Then he heard them.

"Tee-hee!" giggled a voice. Holly imagined that this must be Scraggle-wort.

"Woo hoo!" said a second voice. Hazel-bumpkin, Holly presumed.

"There's *no one* here," said Scraggle-wort, sounding amazed. "Imagine not leaving a

look-out . . . The Flower Fairies really are mind-bogglingly stupid! Ha ha ha ha!"

Holly bristled quietly, but stayed out of sight. So these were the Bad Flower Fairies, were they? Well, they were *very* rude.

"Let's get to work!" said Hazel-bumpkin. "We can mess this place up in a flash. By the time Holly gets back from his Christmas visiting, the Fairy Grotto will be no more. And this time, we'll make a really good job of

it, so there's no chance of rebuilding things before Christmas Eve."

"Ho ho ho," said Scraggle-wort.

"Ho ho ho," repeated Hazel-bumpkin. "You're laughing like Santa Claus. That's great, boss," he said. "Ho ho ho!"

Scraggle-wort was suddenly serious. "Enough of the chuckles," he said. "We've got work to do. We'll start over he— arggghhh!"

The yelp was followed by an "ouch" and then another "ouch". With a grim smile of triumph, Holly dragged Lords-and-Ladies' candle from its hiding place. Its warm, orangey glow lit up the Fairy Grotto. And then Holly got the biggest shock ever. There was no one to be seen.

The Fairy Grotto was totally empty!

Chapter Five
Caught!

Holly scanned the moonlit Fairy Grotto in disbelief. He'd heard the Bad Flower Fairies. They'd walked into his prickly trap. So where *were* they? He jumped at the sound of a muffled squeak, which was followed swiftly by a shushing noise.

"Who's there?" he demanded. Hopping neatly about the leaf-strewn grotto, he waved his berry candle into the darkest corners, hoping to reveal the intruders.

He found no one.

"Ouch!"

Holly whirled round to see a leaf rocking to and fro, as if the breeze were blowing it. But the strangest thing was that there *was* no breeze. And the grotto was still empty . . . This was by far the most peculiar thing that had ever happened to him and he felt puzzled and more than a little nervous.

"Ooooh!" A strange, warbling cry filled the grotto.

At once, Holly knew for certain that someone was playing tricks on him and became very angry. "Just because I can't see you doesn't mean that I don't know you're there!" he roared. "Whoever you are and whatever you're doing, come out *now*!"

"We won't," said a defiant voice. It sounded very much as if it belonged to Hazel-bumpkin. "And you can't see us even

54

if you wanted to, because we're *invisible*!" the voice added triumphantly.

"So there!" added Scraggle-wort.

Of course! It all made sense now. The Bad Fairies had used magic to hide from Holly! Well, they weren't the only ones who could play at *that* game . . . Hurriedly casting his candle to one side, Holly scooped up handfuls of precious dust from the sparkling floor of the grotto. He held his hands behind his back and approached the wibbling leaves.

At the last minute, he threw the fairy dust into the air and uttered the magic words: *Fairy dust, fairy dust, make things sparkly and bright!*

The glittering particles floated downwards, landing on two figures, making them glow as brightly as starlight. Bit by bit, the fairy dust revealed two pointy hats, four long pointy ears, two sets of pointy wings and two raggedy outfits. And the biggest surprise of all was that these were not Flower Fairies at all—bad or otherwise. They were *elves*!

"Ooops," said the smaller elf of the two. "I think we've been found out. What shall we do now, boss?"

"Run!" cried the other elf.

"Er . . . I think it might be best if you told me exactly what you've been up to," said Holly sternly, fluttering quickly across the grotto to block their exit.

So reluctantly, the elves explained. Scraggle-wort and Hazel-bumpkin didn't exist—they were just made-up names. It was

the elves who had spread the rumor about the Bad Flower Fairies. Then, they'd used elfin magic to make themselves invisible before sneaking into the Flower Fairies' Garden and carrying out the mischief.

Who had cast a grumpy spell over the good-natured glow-worms?

The elves.

Who had invaded Holly's Fairy Grotto and messed it all up?

The pesky elves.

They'd invented the new words to Holly's song too.

"But why?" asked the bewildered Flower Fairy.

"Because *we* are the elves," sneered the chief elf. "We don't like Christmas. 'Bah humbug', and all that." He shuddered with distaste.

"Just like the mysterious Bad Flower

Fairies . . ." said Holly, rubbing his chin thoughtfully. "I see."

That evening, a very important meeting took place in the Flower Fairies' Garden. Everyone was invited, from the wise Kingcup and the beautiful Queen of the Meadow to the baby fairies, who yawned politely behind their hands. (It was long past their bedtimes.)

Holly had gathered them all together to tell them what had been going on. It didn't take long.

"So there weren't any Bad Flower Fairies after all?" said gentle Rose. "Well, that's a relief."

"I might have known it was the elves all along," said Dandelion, with a knowing nod. "In fact, if you'd asked me, I could have worked it out for you days ago. I don't have much to do at this time of year, now that my petals have gone and my clocks are empty of seeds . . ." He folded his arms and looked forlorn.

"You can help me sort out the letters to Santa Claus," offered Yew. "I could do with an extra pair of hands."

Dandelion grinned broadly. "Really?" he said. "Excellent! Detective or postman—I don't mind what I do as long as I'm busy!"

Kingcup stood up, towering over the other fairies. He was clad in his usual outfit of shimmering gold, with a crown of yellow flower stamens perched on his golden hair. There were gasps of admiration.

The royal fairy coughed politely. "If we could just return to the matter at hand," he said. "Does anyone have any ideas for how we can deal with the elf situation?"

The crowd of Flower Fairies looked bewildered. This wasn't the sort of thing that usually happened in their lovely garden and no one was quite sure what to suggest.

"I have an idea," said Holly quietly.

He scrambled to his feet and gulped nervously before addressing the others. "Why don't we invite the elves to the Fairy Grotto on Christmas Eve?" he said. "Then we can show them what a wonderful time of year it is. They might even begin to like it."

Some of the fairies looked a little uncertain. The elves were the most mischievous creatures in Flower Fairyland. They'd sabotaged the Fairy Grotto already and they weren't well known for their politeness. Could they be trusted to behave themselves on Christmas Eve? There were mutters from the crowd. Then a small fairy with pale orange wings, wearing a dusky-pink spotted frock, put up her hand.

"Excuse me," said Spindle Berry shyly. "It's the season of goodwill, isn't it? I think they should be invited."

"Quite right!" boomed Kingcup. "Holly's

idea is a splendid one. If everyone is in agreement, let's send one of the crows to invite the elves to the party." He looked around the crowd. "Well?"

There were a few cautious nods.

"Then it's settled," said Kingcup, grinning broadly.

"Anyway, I must fly. I've lots to do before the party . . ." And with a swoosh of his sage-green cloak, he hurried away.

Chapter Six

Christmas Wishes

On Christmas Eve, it got dark sooner than
usual. Clouds rolled in during the day,
covering the winter sky with a thick, grey
blanket. By night-time, the moon was hidden
and Holly had needed extra candles from
Lords-and-Ladies fairy to light the grotto.

"You've surpassed yourself this time,
Holly!" called Almond Blossom as she
arrived and immediately helped herself to
a beechnut of elderberry juice. "It looks
amazing . . . I love Christmas, you know. It

reminds me that spring is just around the corner!"

Holly smiled. "Did you remember your letter to Santa Claus?" he asked.

Almond Blossom patted her skirt pocket. "Safe in here!" she smiled, before skipping away to admire the wonderful festive food.

Before long, the grotto was a-flutter with wings and awash with colorful petals. Almost everyone had arrived. Everyone, that was, except for two very important guests. Holly tutted softly to himself. Where were the elves? They really ought to be here by now. It was almost time to—

Someone *tap-tap-tapped* on Holly's shoulder.

"What?" Holly whirled around to see two oddly dressed characters standing before him. They shifted from one foot to the other, looking very uncomfortable. "What?" Holly repeated, more softly this time.

The two creatures wore bright red tunics with white belts. Their stockings were green and on their feet were pointy green shoes. Each wore a red hat with a white, furry rim and a white bobble on the top. Strangest of all, their faces were hidden by fluffy white beards.

"Isn't it a dress up party?" asked the

taller of the two new arrivals, in a very grumpy voice. "We thought we had to wear costumes . . ."

"Oh . . ." said Holly, suddenly realizing who he was speaking to. "You're the elves!" He had an urge to giggle and only kept a straight face with the greatest difficulty.

"So why isn't anyone else dressed up?" demanded the taller elf. "We thought that all Christmas parties were dress up." He paused and scratched his beard. "That's one of the reasons we don't like Christmas, you see. We don't like dressing up."

"Cotton-Grass fairy gave us the fluff for our beards. It's really itchy," added the smaller elf. "We feel silly."

"Well, it isn't actually dress up," said Holly, "but you look amazing! You're dressed as Santa Claus' elves, right?"

They nodded glumly.

"You must come and join the party at once," said Holly, feeling sorry for the two forlorn elves. Suddenly, it didn't matter at all that they'd tried to wreck the Fairy Grotto. He just wanted these mischievous creatures to cheer up and enjoy Christmas as much as everyone else.

"There's one more thing," said the taller elf. "We're, er . . . That is to say, sss . . . sss . . ." He puffed out a great plume of air and tried again. "Sss—"

"Sorry," interrupted the smaller elf. "We're sorry for messing up your grotto."

"Oh, don't give it another thought," said kind-hearted Holly. "Come and join in the fun!"

So they did. Nervously at first, and then—when they realized that all the Flower Fairies thought they were good sports for dressing up—more confidently, they weaved among

the crowd, admiring
the decorations and
making new fairy
friends.

Before long, the party
was in full swing. Honeysuckle
and Ragged Robin had brought their
instruments and carol music played softly in
the background. The younger Flower Fairies
gazed in awe at the glow-worms, who had
balanced among the twigs and branches of
Holly's tree—they looked just like the fairy

lights that twinkled
through the windows
of the house at the
end of the Flower
Fairies' Garden.

Ding-dong-ding! Ding-dong-ding! Ding-dong-ding!

The sound of Canterbury Bell fairy's large
mauve bells jangled merrily throughout the
Fairy Grotto, interrupting conversations
and telling all the fairies that a very special
ceremony was about to take place.

Holly grinned with glee as Queen of the Meadow swooped into the grotto on the back of a sleek swallow. A cloud of flaxen hair framed her fine features. She wore an ivory gown, while a necklace of large, green pearls hung around her neck. In her hand was a silken purse. The queen climbed down gracefully from the bird's back and smiled at the Flower Fairies. "I think you all know why I'm here," she said softly.

There was a sea of bobbing heads as the fairies nodded. The two elves looked at each other, totally bewildered.

"It's time to send our letters to Santa Claus," Queen of the Meadow announced, to huge applause. "Now, don't be shy," she said.

One by one, the Flower Fairies came forward and placed their letters on the sparkly ground before the queen. Instead of parchment, each fairy had used a petal or a leaf from his or her own plant. Soon, a multicolored heap lay at Queen of the Meadow's feet.

"Is that all?" she asked, when no one else stepped forward.

At once, Holly realized that the two elves had not brought letters. Hurriedly, he went to whisper in the queen's ear.

"Ah," she said. Quickly searching among the folds of her gown, the beautiful fairy produced two leaves from her own flower and a feathery quill pen. Then she scribbled a message on each leaf and balanced them on top of the pile. "I have written a Christmas wish for each of our two guests," she explained.

The two elves smiled happily.

"And now for some Flower Fairy magic!" said Queen of the Meadow. She delved into her silken purse and pulled out a handful of sparkling fairy dust. This she sprinkled over the heap of letters, chanting: "*Fairy dust, fairy dust, fly to Santa tonight!*"

Slowly, the petals and leaves lifted into the air, flapping gracefully as they rose higher and higher. For a few moments, the air swirled with color—and then the letters were gone.

"Ooooooooh," chorused the elves. "That

was wonderful!" And then something even more wonderful happened.

It began to snow.

Softly at first, and then with increasing speed, tiny white flakes fell from the sky, cloaking Holly's berries and leaves with a layer of sparkling white. Now the Fairy Grotto looked even more beautiful than before. Within seconds, everyone was

playing in the snow.

"What did you write in the elves' letters?" Holly whispered to Queen of the Meadow.

She smiled. "I simply asked that the elves should enjoy Christmas as much as we do," she whispered back. "I think it worked, don't you?"

Holly caught sight of the two elves. Their faces were glowing with happiness as they built a snowman that looked remarkably like Holly himself. He chuckled. Everyone—and that meant Flower Fairies and elves—was having a simply marvellous time.

"Merry Christmas!" he cried. "Merry Christmas, everyone!"

The Magical Christmas Discovery

By Pippa Le Quesne

Contents

Chapter One

The Mystery Begins

"Burdock!"

Coming out of
an elegant spin, the
Christmas Tree Fairy
glided to a halt and called
out to her friend, "Let's
skate together."

Burdock grinned and
gave a thumbs-up from
the other side of the

frozen pond, where he had been practicing
his speed skating. Then he put his head
down and accelerated towards her, his russet
wings flattened against his back. He was
about to whizz past when he grabbed her

hand at the last minute. "Gotcha!" he yelled, as the two of them zoomed across the ice.

Christmas giggled with delight as they fell into step, their waxed-leaf boots barely skimming the surface as they skated faster and faster, until their surroundings became a blur.

"On three, open your wings," Burdock said breathlessly, and Christmas squeezed his hand in response. "One ... two ... three!"

As they opened their wings in unison, the momentum propelled the little Flower Fairies into the air, where they twisted off in opposite directions, laughing gleefully.

"Hey, you two!" came a friendly shout, from nearby. "I was wondering where you'd gone."

Hearing the familiar voice, both Burdock and Christmas changed tack in mid-air and fluttered over to the yew tree, where

Yew himself sat astride one of the spindly branches. As they landed next to him, panting for breath, he clapped his hands in appreciation.

"Fantastic show! And I especially liked your finale." Yew beamed. "Now, you must be dying for a cup of tea. Make yourself comfortable and I'll be back with refreshments."

Christmas, who was used to the spiky needles of her own tree, felt quite at home amidst the spirals of dark green leaves, but Burdock was a bit more cautious about getting settled. However, he soon discovered that the glossy leaves were softer than they appeared, and it was not long before the three friends were sipping warming rosehip tea and enthusiastically discussing the upcoming festivities.

Yew lived in the Flower Fairies' Garden, and Burdock and Christmas, who came from the wayside and woodland, had come to visit him—as well as to go skating on the garden pond.

"Mmm, I can't believe it's the day after tomorrow," Burdock commented, chewing busily on a piece of candied ginger.

"I know," Christmas responded, feeling a bit giddy at the thought. "Has Holly got the grove ready yet?" She directed her question at Yew.

"Oh, haven't you heard?" He raised a quizzical eyebrow. "He's not decorating the holly bush this year. We've all decided to come to the woods instead."

"Wh-what?" stuttered Christmas, almost spilling her tea in surprise. Then, looking from one friend to the other, she caught sight of Burdock's smirk and noticed that Yew was also having trouble suppressing a grin. He let out a peal of laughter.

"You are so mischievous, teasing me like that!" Christmas exclaimed, turning pink with embarrassment. She concentrated hard on smoothing down the layers of her white net skirt, until her cheeks had stopped burning.

Each year, on Christmas Day, Yew and all the other Garden Flower Fairies centered their celebrations around the holly bush, whereas the Wild Fairies gathered in the woodlands and held their party under the boughs of Christmas's fir tree. She'd always felt honored to have been chosen to be the hostess but, as her closest friends knew, she also put a lot of pressure on herself to make each year extra special.

"Ahem," Christmas said, clearing her throat, once she'd stopped blushing.

"Actually, Yew, I was going to ask you if we could take some of your berries back with us? They're so pretty and they always add a nice splash of color to the tree."

"Yes, of course. Help yourselves," replied Yew, proudly gesturing to the reddish-pink fruit that nestled among the branches.

"There's a nice batch up at the top."

"I'll go and pick them," Burdock volunteered. "It's not often that I get to have such a great view of the garden." Pushing his untidy auburn hair out of his eyes, he scrambled to his feet.

"Fantastic," said Christmas, unhooking her conker-shell basket from a branch and handing it to him. "Then, we'll have another

cup of tea and start thinking creatively!"

Burdock hadn't been gone for very long, and Christmas and Yew had only just started discussing garlands and baubles, when a shout came from higher up the tree.

It was Burdock.

Yew jumped to his feet. "What did he say?"

Suddenly there was a rustling sound above their heads and Burdock poked his head down through the branches. "I said— quick! Come up here, right away." And he disappeared from view.

"He's probably bumped into Robin Redbreast, or spotted the cat playing in the

garden," Christmas commented, as the two friends nimbly leapt from one springy branch to the next.

But when they caught up with him, the expression on his face told them otherwise. Usually rosy-cheeked, Burdock's complexion was ashen and the twinkle had gone right out of his eyes. Something was definitely wrong. Turning to Christmas, he put a hand on her arm and said very seriously, "Take a deep breath and look over towards the house. But make sure you hold on tightly to something . . ."

Chapter Two

Fairy with a Mission

Christmas hadn't noticed that her hands
were clenched into fists, as if she were
still gripping on to the yew branch. While
her friends had helped her down to the
ground, she'd just concentrated on slowing
her breathing. Now, as Burdock began to
massage her hands and Yew went to fetch
a blanket, Christmas felt flutters of panic
rising in her chest again.

"What could they want with one of my trees?" she said in a trembling voice. An image of the humans carrying the beautiful fir into their house flashed through her mind, and she shuddered. "And how will it survive . . . in a container?"

"Calm down, Christmas. We'll work it all out," Yew said kindly. He'd returned with an acorn cup of soothing chamomile tea and a moss blanket.

"Don't worry about the container," Burdock added. "Remember when the humans planted lots of Geranium's flowers in earthenware pots? She was really worried too, but soon learned that as long as they're surrounded by earth and get lots of water then they positively thrive."

"You're right." Christmas smiled weakly. "And they did seem to be carrying it very carefully," she added bravely.

"Not just that," said Yew, straightening his jaunty green hat, "but we all know how much these humans love plants and trees. They must be taking it indoors to admire it . . . or perhaps they think it needs some extra warmth while it's this cold outside?"

"But fir trees *love* the cold." Christmas shook her head, dark blonde tresses of hair falling either side of her heart-shaped face. "No, there's only one thing for it. I shall have

to go into the house and make sure that no
harm comes to my tree!"

Burdock gasped and dropped the shiny
yew berry that he had been absentmindedly
passing from one hand to the other. "You
can't do that! You know we're not allowed
inside the house."

Yew nodded vigorously. "Flower Fairy
Law absolutely forbids it, Christmas. You
know that you mustn't risk being seen by a
human—for all of our sakes."

"I know," Christmas replied. "It's just . . .
I can't stand by and do nothing. Flower Fairy
Law also says that we have to protect our
plants at all costs." There were tears in her
eyes as she addressed her two friends. "And,
as Kingcup and Queen of the Meadow are in
the middle of their hibernation and I can't ask
their permission, I shall just have to make
my own judgement. And, I think, as long as

I'm very careful, they would want me to take the risk . . ." The dainty little fairy slipped the moss blanket off her shoulders and got to her feet. "I've made my mind up. After dark—when everyone's asleep—I'm going to investigate!"

* * *

The garden looked so beautiful in the moonlight. Although it was midwinter and most of the fairies and their flowers were hibernating, there was still plenty of plant life. As well as the elegant yew tree which swayed and rustled in the light wind, the spiky leaves of the holly bush threw fantastic

shadows across the lawn.

Once Christmas had made her decision about venturing into the house, she had taken a nap. It seemed like a good idea after the events of the afternoon, plus she wanted to be well rested and alert for nightfall. Burdock had returned to the woods to check on the other fir trees, and Yew had kept a look out

while Christmas was sleeping. Then, when the house was quiet and the lights had all been turned off, he'd woken her up and wished her luck. "If you're not back by this time tomorrow night, then I'll organize a search party," Yew said, before kissing her on the cheek and heading off to bed himself.

Now Christmas stood staring up at the house and trying to figure out how to get in. There were no open windows and she felt sure that even someone as slight as herself couldn't squeeze in under the back door. *There must be a way*, she thought, rubbing her hands together to keep warm.

Curiosity had got the better of nearly all of the Flower Fairies at one time or another and most of them had had a quick peek through a window. But as far as Christmas knew, no one had ever been *in* before. She gulped, trying to suppress the

nerves fluttering up inside her. Then, she remembered her poor fir tree trapped inside and immediately her determination came flooding back. It had to be rescued—the problem was, how?

She was still wondering what to do, when she heard a *thump* that brought her to her senses. This was closely followed by the sight of two large, emerald green eyes glowing in the dark. Christmas's heart began pounding hard inside her chest and her hands became clammy with fear. An animal had jumped over the wall and was now padding up the path in front of her! Staying as still as she could, she scrutinized the black silhouette. All of a sudden, it came to her—she

recognized that long waving tail with its snowy-white tip and four matching paws. It was the cat!

The little Tree Fairy's first instinct was to flee and, opening her wings, she was about to take flight when she spotted something that stopped her in her tracks.

The cat—who, luckily, hadn't caught sight

of her—had settled down beside the back door and was occupied with grooming itself. What Christmas had seen, now that her eyes had adjusted properly to the dark, was a square flap cut into the human door. And, if she wasn't mistaken, judging by the size of it, it had to be for the cat. So, sooner or later, when the creature tired of washing its paws, it would push it open. Which meant that, if Christmas was very careful, it could prove to be precisely the way into the house that she was looking for!

Chapter Three
A Narrow Escape

It felt as though hours had passed rather than minutes when the cat finally got to its feet. Christmas had flown as near to the animal as she dared and was crouched behind a plant pot, poised for action. Now the cat was stretching.

"Right, it's now or never," the brave Tree Fairy whispered into the cold air. Her stomach was doing somersaults at the thought of flying just a hair's breadth behind the cat's tail as she passed through the flap. Taking a deep breath to steady her nerves, she braced herself for flight.

"This is it!" Christmas sprang silently from the ground and rapidly flapped her wings so that she hovered as close to the door as she dared, just hidden by the shadows. Then, at the same moment as the cat shoved the flap with a paw and tucked its head down to push its way through, Christmas straightened her arms out in front of her, and with her wings folded against her back,

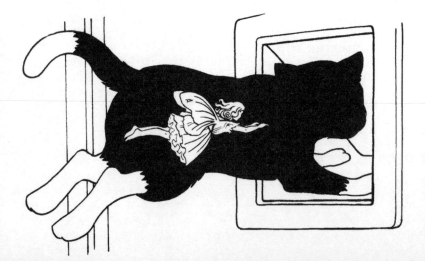

dived in after it.

As she fell through the other side and her hands hit the mat, she tucked her legs up under her and let the forward motion carry her into a somersault. Over and over she went, until after the third tumble she came to an abrupt halt on her bottom.

I did it! Christmas congratulated herself as she glanced around. She had landed in a hallway that went from the back to the front of the house and had several doors leading off it on each side. Everything was so

enormous compared to her, and so different from anything in Flower Fairyland. *Wow, I'm actually in the human house*, she thought to herself, feeling a thrill of excitement.

Now, where could they have put that tree of mine? Full of adrenalin from her successful entrance, her mind began to race on to the next part of her mission.

But she had only just got to her feet and was busy dusting herself off when she heard the clicking of claws on the hard wooden floor. Christmas's heart missed a beat. When they had first come through the flap, the cat had darted off into one of the other rooms but, now, she was horrified to look up and see it standing in a doorway further down the hall. And there was no doubt about it—the animal had seen her and was ready to pounce!

Christmas soared up into the air and shot through the doorway of the nearest room,

frantically searching for a surface to land on
that would be too high for the cat to jump
on to. However, the agile creature wasn't far
behind and over her shoulder Christmas
watched it spring on to a bookcase, where it
could easily launch itself from. She *had* to get
out of there. But now, if she flew too close,
there was the risk of being swiped at by an
outstretched paw. Panicking, the terrified
fairy beat her wings as hard as she could and
headed back out into the hall, keeping as

close to the ceiling as possible
and giving the cat a wide berth.

Her wings were aching terribly and
she knew that no matter how much she
needed to stay air-bound, it wouldn't be
long before they gave out entirely. "You can
do it," Christmas said out loud through
gritted teeth. "There's got to be something
in this next room." And summoning her
last reserves of energy, she flew through the
adjacent doorway.

The sight that met her eyes made her heart
soar, and the overwhelmed fairy almost

dropped to the floor with joy. For there, in the middle of the room, standing majestically straight and tall, was the potted fir tree!

When she reached the very top of the tree, Christmas let herself relax a little. There was nothing in the room that was nearly as high and the spindly branches of the fir would never support the cat's weight. Also, because

it was firmly planted in a large tub of earth, no matter how many times the cat tapped at its base, it would remain upright. And there wasn't a chance that she was coming down— even if it stayed on guard all night!

However, Christmas didn't have to wait long before the cat appeared to have worked this out for itself and, either bored with the game or lured by the thought of a cosy chair to curl up in, it sauntered away, flicking its tail huffily as it went.

A combination of exhaustion and relief washed over Christmas, and burying her face in the soft fragrant needles, she allowed herself to close her eyes. *Just for a minute*, she told herself. But within seconds, with her arms wrapped securely round her beloved tree, the little Tree Fairy had drifted off to sleep.

Chapter Four
A Wonderful Discovery

"Look! Esta—look up there!"

Christmas came to, with a start. Where was she?

"What—where? I can't see," said another voice.

"On top of the tree—that beautiful fairy."

Christmas's eyes flew open. She had woken at the top of a fir—not unusual, but she was in a *room*, and two human girls were staring up at her.

"She's lovely," Esta said.

"Mom must have put her there to surprise us," the elder child replied. "She could do with a little fixing up—and a wand. When Mom wakes up we'll get her down."

"Good idea. And let's find the decorations. Ooh, I can't believe it's Christmas Day tomorrow!" Esta spun around in excitement before running out of the room. Her big sister followed, giggling with pleasure.

Once she was sure that they had definitely left, Christmas exhaled.

Her immediate response had been to hold her breath and not move a muscle. Then she'd hoped against hope that because she was far above them, they wouldn't notice the fact that she was actually *real* and not a doll fairy. So far so good.

"But I can't possibly hold my breath every time they appear. And pretty soon they're going to get me down to smarten me up." She shuddered at the thought of what would happen if they realized she was alive. "What am I going to do?"

Christmas wracked her brains for an answer. Of course she could try and escape from the house unnoticed, but then what about her tree? Having got this far without coming to harm it would be a dreadful waste to leave before she'd worked out a way to rescue the fir. She hadn't even found out why the humans had brought it into the house in the first place. There had to be another solution. If only she could make the children believe that she was actually a doll . . .

"Maybe I can," Christmas suddenly said out loud. Then thrusting a hand in her skirt pockets she pulled out a neatly folded petal handkerchief and opened it carefully. There in the center was a mound of gleaming particles. Fairy dust.

Muffled voices alerted her to the fact that she didn't have much time before the children came back, so, taking a handful of the magic powder, she threw it over herself and quickly thought up a spell.

"Fairy dust, fairy dust, work your charm. Keep me still as a doll and safe from harm!"

As Christmas said the words, the dust began to sparkle and dance.

It's working, she thought to herself. As it settled on her, she became aware of a tranquil sensation that gradually spread from her feet, up through her legs and down her arms, until it had reached her fingertips. And, at that moment, when the two girls came bursting into the room with their mother, the fairy on top of the tree was impossible to tell apart from a doll.

Christmas was having a splendid time. Once she realized that the humans were totally unaware that she was a living fairy, she relaxed and started to enjoy her window into their world. She'd been pleasantly surprised to discover that they too celebrated the festive season. She'd never really given much thought to whether Flower Fairies and human beings had similar traditions. But they certainly did—and the most wonderful one of all was that they also decorated a fir tree with pretty ornaments and lights and called it a Christmas tree!

Christmas sighed with pleasure. It was such a relief to know that they meant the fir no harm. On the contrary, they were treating it with real care and appreciation and spending a lot of time deciding how it should look. *Just like I do*, she thought to herself.

However, the notion of choosing the

perfect decorations shattered her daydream.
Today was Christmas Eve and her fir trees
in the forest stood bare of trimmings. She
wasn't even nearly ready for Christmas Day
and all the Wild Fairies were relying on her
to make theirs extra special! Not just that,
but she still wasn't sure what the humans

were going to do with their tree once the
celebrations were over. It was all very well
for it to live in a tub for a short period of
time, but it needed to spread its roots and

grow, and it would be stifled in such a small container.

Christmas's heart sank. She needed a plan. But even if she came up with one, there was nothing she could do while the humans were about and she had to stay frozen. Her only chance was after dark once they had gone to bed. And that meant finding a way to get a message to Yew to tell him that she needed to stay for a little longer. For, unless she let him know before nightfall that she was perfectly safe, he would probably lead a whole army of Flower Fairies into the house, and then she would be putting everyone in danger.

Chapter Five

Christmas Magic!

Luckily for Christmas, the two girls were ushered into bed early with the promise of Santa Claus leaving presents if they were fast asleep when he came. And not long after, their parents retired upstairs too, knowing that the following morning would be an early start for them all. So, when they shut the sitting-room door and left the little Tree Fairy to her own devices, she still had plenty of time to think of a way to contact Yew.

The fairy-dust

charm had begun to wear off and already Christmas could feel her fingers and toes coming back to life. In one hand, she was now holding a delicate green wand with a gold star, and on her head she wore a matching headband with a pearly white star in its center. Both were gifts from Freya, the eldest girl, who had spent the afternoon carefully making them. Then, ever so gently, she had combed Christmas's hair, puffed up her frilly

skirts, and re-tied the simple green sash that crossed over her chest and around her waist.

"Perfect!" she had said, passing the fairy to her mother to position on the top of the tree. "And you can do real magic now that you've got a wand," she whispered before going up to bed.

Christmas smiled at the thought of the kind child, and holding out her arm, which had just become mobile again, tapped the wand on a string of beads draped on the branches below her.

"Change!" she commanded, not expecting anything to happen but having a bit of fun.

But before her very eyes, the beads began to

shimmer, and then to glow a brilliant red. "What's happening?" she asked in wonderment.

She didn't have to wait long to find out, as moments later the brightness had faded and the beads became softer and plumper and some of them changed to a dusky pink. They reminded her of something ... Bending down to take a closer look, Christmas gasped. For the beads had turned into a string of beautiful shiny yew berries!

"Surely not?" the Tree Fairy said quizzically, as she examined the wand in her hand.

Then, she held it at arm's length once more and tapped a rope of tinsel. "Change!" she repeated.

And within seconds, the metallic decoration had turned into twists of pale yellow catkins—identical to the ones that hung on the Hazel-Catkin fairy's tree.

"It's incredible!" Christmas exclaimed. Then, alighting from her perch, she began

to fly up and down and around the tree, touching each and every bauble and trinket and turning them from something manmade into something of natural beauty. She turned glass ornaments into snow-encrusted pine cones or pretty plane-tree balls; she turned the colored lights into strings of vivid yellow winter jasmine flowers; and finally, she covered the tree in small red candles just like the ones that Lords-and-Ladies left in the garden.

When she flew back to admire her handiwork, she couldn't help but feel pride swelling in her chest. "Freya was right. Now, I really can create magic!" The fir tree really did look amazing.

Landing on the window ledge to catch her breath, the Tree Fairy turned the wand over in her hands to examine it properly. It was very odd—it just looked like a piece of painted wood with some gold paper on top, but somehow it had given her newfound abilities. Of course, all the Flower Fairies had their own special fairy dust, which they made from grinding up pollen or seeds from

their particular plant, but it didn't have a huge amount of power. It was considered a helping hand in times of need and had to be used sparingly during the course of the year, until Mother Nature provided the means to create a new batch. Christmas gazed out into the garden fondly. As her eyes wandered across the lawn, she caught sight of the yew tree and suddenly her memory was jogged.

"Yew!" she squeaked. "He'll be on his way any minute. And I need to get a message to him." Glancing down at the wand again, a thought suddenly occurred to her. "I wonder . . ."

Then raising it upright and standing to face the window, she began swirling it in a complicated pattern. "Make me some words!" she commanded, and straightaway, the letters that she had

written in the air began to sparkle on the glass in front of her. *I'm safe and I'll be there soon*, her message to Yew read.

"That ought to do it," Christmas said, feeling rather pleased. "Now . . ."

Sitting back down on the window ledge, she turned her attention to the fir tree and tried to work out how to complete her task. She had certainly created a special bit of Christmas magic to say thank you to the humans for taking good care of her tree, but somehow she needed to convince them that once the festive season was over they needed to return it to its natural habitat.

"Maybe seeing it like this will be enough," the little Tree Fairy murmured, swinging her legs as she thought. "Or do they need it spelled out to them?"

Suddenly, Christmas laughed out loud. She'd got it!

"I'll leave Yew's message a bit longer to make sure he's seen it, and then I'll spell it out for them." She hugged herself in delight. "It'll be perfect—I'll write 'PLANT ME' in nice big glittery letters. And if that doesn't work, nothing will!"

Chapter Six
Home Sweet Home

Christmas opened her eyes and yawned.
Despite there being a frost on the ground,
a warm feeling spread all over her—it was
Christmas Day and she was back in the
woods!

By the time she'd dropped in on Yew to let
him know that she was safely home, it had
been late into the night.
But she was far too
excited to stay in bed
this morning. Besides,
she'd had a far more
comfortable sleep in her
hammock, compared to
the night in the house

when she'd clung to the top of the tree in fear
of the cat. Anyway, there was work to do!

Grabbing a large hazelnut from a satchel
that was hooked over a branch, Christmas
opened her wings and let herself glide
to the forest floor. *Thank you so much,*
Burdock, she thought, taking a
big bite out of the nut, and
inspecting the neat piles
that he'd left at the
base of the fir.

Her dear friend must have worked feverishly. For there was every decoration she could want to make sure this year's Christmas tree looked as fantastic as ever.

"Right," she said, hauling a heavy garland of catkins over her shoulder, "let's start from the bottom up."

Close by, a blackbird was warbling a carol, and Christmas hummed as she moved round the tree. Picking up first a string of burdock burs, followed by a sprig of holly, and then some fluffy cotton-grass, she took her time to carefully consider what looked best and where each decoration should be placed. It was hard work, but the cheerful

Tree Fairy was in her element. When all that remained to be done was to add one last finishing touch, she decided to take a break.

"Phew!" Christmas said, perching herself on a toadstool and casting her eye over the fir tree, resplendent in all its trimming. She chuckled to herself as she thought about how quickly she could have finished if she'd used the wand that Freya had given her. But on her return journey from the garden, just hours

before, she had given it considerable thought.

The easy thing to do would have been to take a nice long nap before decorating the tree, as it would have taken no more than a few taps of the magic wand to complete the task. She had been tempted—but only for the briefest of moments. After all, what she enjoyed most about Christmas Day was giving to others—and it was a real pleasure to see her friends' faces light up when they first

caught sight of the tree. It was always worth all the effort.

No, once she had used its powers to help her open the cat flap so that she could leave the human house, she had promised herself that she would only allow herself one more wish. Then she would put it away somewhere and treasure it—but not use it. In fact she wasn't even going to mention it to anyone else. She had a gut feeling that it would be better—not just for her, but for all of Flower Fairyland—if her life just had the same amount of enchantment as everyone else's.

"No one open your eyes until I say the word," Christmas called to the assembled fairies, who she'd given strict instructions to gather beside the wild cherry tree and wait for her there.

Then picking up the wand, one last time,

she flew to the top of the fir, where she'd
fashioned a star, and hovered in front of it.
She had made it out of the bendy branches of
winter jasmine which were leafless but had
little yellow star-shaped flowers dotted all
over them. It looked beautiful already, but
Christmas had plans to add a bit more magic.

"Change!" she whispered, giving it a tap.
And just as she had hoped, the decoration
began to shimmer and glow until it was

shining bright like one of the stars straight out of the night sky. It was perfect.

Christmas took a deep breath and tucked the wand back into the folds of her dress. "OK—everyone—I'm ready!"

Then one by one, with a tremendous amount of ooh-ing and aah-ing, the Flower Fairies of the Wayside and Woodland made their way towards the Christmas tree to begin the festivities.

Christmas didn't think that her day could get much better, but she was wrong.

After they'd all exchanged presents and feasted on a whole array of goodies such as warm walnut bread and apple and caramel cake, the fairies had sung carols and played several rounds of charades. Everyone had said how good it was to have her back and how brave she'd been to go into the house,

but most of all they complimented her on the special star that shone on top of the tree.

Then, she and Burdock had decided to go and visit the Garden Fairies' Christmas Grotto, and now they were standing in front of the house with Yew. For no sooner had they joined him and his friends for a glass of punch under the holly bush, than he'd whisked them away. "I've got something to show you," he'd whispered into Christmas's ear as he led her up the garden.

"What is it?" Christmas wondered out loud, glancing at Burdock to see if it was one of their jokes at her expense. But he appeared to be totally in the dark too.

"It's a surprise," Yew replied, when he'd stopped directly in front of the house.
He pointed towards a window. "If I'm not

mistaken, that's meant for you?"

Christmas looked up to where he was indicating. And there, stuck to the glass, was a piece of paper with big squiggly writing all over it. *Dear Fairy*, read the first line. It was a letter. "Will one of you read it to me, please?" she said in a small voice, completely taken aback.

Yew nodded and cleared his throat:

"Dear Fairy

Thank you for turning our Christmas tree into the prettiest one that we've ever had. We still don't know where you came from or where you are now, but we loved meeting you. And we promise that we will plant this tree back in the garden next week and make sure that every one we have from now on is returned to the wild.

Have a very Merry Christmas!

Love Freya and Esta xxx"

By the time Yew had finished, there were big fat tears rolling down Christmas's cheeks, but she was smiling. They were tears of happiness. *We will, Freya, we will*, she said silently to herself, wishing them the same.

"You did it!" yelled Burdock suddenly, dancing a little celebratory jig on the spot.

"I know!" Christmas beamed. "And it's the best present *ever*!" Then, wiping her eyes, she put an arm around each of her friends'

shoulders and hugged them to her. "Come on, boys—let's go skating. I'll race you to the pond!" And without waiting for either of them to reply, she sped off towards the frozen pond, shrieking with joyful laughter.

Snowdrop's Winter Wonderland

By Pippa Le Quesne

Contents

Chapter One
Hide-and-Seek

Snowdrop turned over on to her left side and, as was her habit, half-opened one eye just in case it was *time*. This wasn't the first occasion that she'd stirred in the last few days but, somehow, something definitely felt different. The hollow of the tree trunk, where the little Flower Fairy had spent the winter months sleeping, was still in semi-darkness, so it couldn't have been a change in the light that had woken her. Shaking her head, she pulled the warm moss blanket up over her ears and tried to settle down again. But, suddenly,

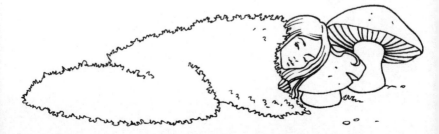

she felt a tingling sensation in the tips of her toes and it grew stronger with every passing second.

Snowdrop sat up and rubbed her eyes. She *knew* that feeling. And it could only mean one thing. Getting to her feet, she patiently spent a few minutes stretching. Then, after opening and closing her pearly white wings a couple of times, she scrambled up the gentle slope to the entrance.

"Ooooh." The little Flower Fairy exhaled with pleasure. She had been right. Although she could only really make out shapes in the half-light of the new day, there was no mistaking the white glow of the nodding flower heads. "You're here!" Snowdrop laughed and dropped lightly to the ground, looping an arm around one of the slender green stalks and swinging herself round happily.

Unlike most of the other Flower Fairies
that slept through the colder months, it
wasn't a change in the weather that roused
her from her sleep. No, Snowdrop woke
when her hardy little plants bravely pushed
their way up through the frozen ground, and
her toes started tingling to alert her of their
arrival!

"I was just about to come and wake you!"
called a cheerful voice from above.

Snowdrop looked up to see one of the boy

Flower Fairies poking his head out between the small glossy leaves of a nearby hedge. It was Box Tree!

She grinned as her friend landed on the ground in front of her and wrapped his arms around her waist. Box Tree was shorter and plumper than Snowdrop, who was tall and willowy, but they were great friends. Together with Winter Jasmine, they were inseparable in the early months of the year when nearly all of Flower Fairyland was still asleep and the garden was very quiet.

"Your flowers came out just this morning,"

Box went on, "and I was determined to be
the first to let you know. But don't tell me—it
was those magic toes of yours, right?"

"I'm afraid so." Snowdrop giggled. "It's so
good to see you," she said, giving him a final
squeeze. "Now, what have you been up to
since I last saw you?"

"Oh, you know, the usual—Christmas, and
seeing the New Year in," replied Box Tree,
with a twinkle in his eye.

Snowdrop sighed. "I so wish that, just

once, I could see what Christmas is like."

"Well, you'll have to try harder to stay awake!" Box teased her, revealing big dimples in his chubby cheeks.

His plant was an evergreen, which meant that he was busy looking after it all year round, and Winter Jasmine's yellow flowers graced the garden at Christmas, so neither of Snowdrop's friends hibernated. Sometimes she felt as though she missed out on lots of fun, but then she did have a very special job . . . Her flowers were the first of the year to bloom and they were an important symbol of hope to all who lived in the garden, reminding them that spring was on its way.

All of a sudden, Snowdrop had a tremendous desire to go exploring—it had been such a long time since she'd seen anything other than the cosy inside of the tree trunk and the pale sun was properly out now.

"Come on!" she said to Box Tree, turning on her heel. "I want to look around and I want to go *everywhere*!"

During the summer, the wall at the end of the garden was a magnificent sight—swathed in climbing sweet peas in delicate shades of pinks and purples. However, when the frost began to bite and it was bare of any foliage, one of the side walls leading up to the house had all the glory. Here, a thick layer of winter jasmine grew and once its summer leaves had been shed, its bright yellow flowers blossomed—providing a permanent ray of sunshine on even the greyest days.

Winter Jasmine was like that too—in dashing yellow stockings, boots and matching hat, he was always sunny and full of life. He had been delighted to see Snowdrop, and had offered her a warming cup of tea immediately. "Time for a game of hide-and-seek," he announced after a few minutes of chatting, draining his acorn cup. "You can do the searching, Snowdrop. Running about will warm you up."

Without waiting for a reply, he darted into the thicket and disappeared from sight. Box Tree raised an eyebrow at Snowdrop. "Right," he said, clambering to his feet and swigging back the last of his elderberry tea.

Snowdrop laughed. It was good to be awake and spending time with her friends.

But goodness, it felt chilly—even for this time of year. She hugged herself, wrapping her bare arms in the soft white cape that was attached to her smock dress. Her flaxen hair was thick and long and she'd never felt the need for a hat, *but I could definitely do with some boots like Winter Jasmine's* she thought, as she began to count out loud.

Snowdrop was feeling quite hot and flustered now, having searched high and low for her two friends. She'd started off with a quick glance in the winter jasmine bush, but there was no sign of either of them. Then, she'd trotted off down the garden and looked in all the usual hiding places that she could think of, but they were nowhere to be seen. So now she was back where she'd started, having a more thorough search.

The bedraggled Flower Fairy parted the twiggy branches of the bush and peered into the undergrowth. She heard a rustling sound.

"Winter Jasmine—is that you?" she whispered, as it dawned on her how well he'd be hidden among his own flowers. In the

gloomy light, she could see what looked like a heap of tangled branches, and *something* was definitely moving there. Realizing that Winter Jasmine was not going to give himself up, Snowdrop crept forward, hoping to surprise him.

Chink, chink.

Snowdrop nearly jumped out of her skin. *What on earth was that?*

Chink chink.

It was loud and shrill and coming from directly in front of her. It sounded like a warning call from a bird or animal in distress. Standing stock-still, she stared. And, when she became accustomed to the dim light, she found that, sure enough, she was looking directly into the beady eye of a female blackbird!

Chapter Two
An Important Promise

"It's all right—I won't hurt you," the gentle Flower Fairy said, tentatively stretching out a hand. She'd yelped in surprise and given the bird a fright. "W-what are you doing here?" she asked as an afterthought. It was strange to see a bird in an enclosed space and she wondered if a cat was on the prowl.

"I'm nesting," the blackbird tweeted nervously. "My mate went off to fetch some food . . . but he's been gone for ages."

Like many of the Flower Fairies,
Snowdrop knew how to converse with the
birds that lived in the garden, even though
they spoke their own language.

"Oh, I see." Sure enough, now she looked
properly, she *could* see that what she'd
mistaken for a pile of twigs was actually a
messy-looking nest. And just peeping out
from beneath the blackbird's dappled brown
feathers were four blue-grey eggs.

"Wow!" Snowdrop exclaimed. It was early even for blackbirds to be rearing their young, and she had never been this close to a bird's nest before. "They're beautiful," she added, resisting the urge to reach out and touch one. The blackbird dipped her head in acknowledgement, before Snowdrop continued eagerly, "If you're hungry, I could watch your eggs while you go off and find some food..."

"Thank you," the bird replied. "But it's not as simple as that." She opened her wings ever so slightly and shifted her weight, as if trying to get comfortable. "From the moment they are laid, either my mate or I have to sit on them to keep them warm—right up until they start to hatch. And we take turns to collect food." Snowdrop nodded in response. "But unless I eat something soon, I'll be so hungry that I won't even be able to keep myself warm, let alone the eggs."

"Oh, golly," responded the little Flower Fairy, beginning to understand the gravity of the problem. She thought for a minute then added, "Do you like nuts and berries? Winter Jasmine—the fairy that lives in this bush—is bound to have some. I could go and fetch a few, if you do."

"That would be marvellous!" The big brown bird warbled with gratitude.

"OK. I'll be back as quickly as possible." Snowdrop smiled reassuringly at the blackbird, who already looked perkier at the prospect of food. Then turning on her heel,

she called over her shoulder, "Everything is going to be all right – I promise."

Wearily, Snowdrop crawled along on her hands and knees, pushing the walnut shell along in front of her. She had been back and forth so many times now that she'd created a tunnel through the center of the bush, ending at the blackbird's nest.

After making her promise, Snowdrop had tirelessly gathered food for her new friend. Wondering where she'd gone, it hadn't been long before Box Tree and Winter Jasmine had come back to find her, and quickly she'd

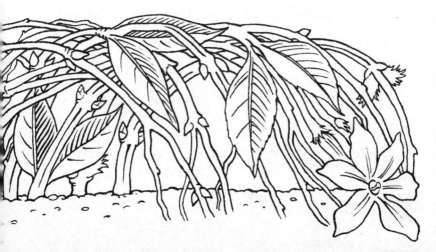

enlisted their help. Being such generous
Flower Fairies, they'd each fetched what they
could spare from their winter supplies and
Snowdrop had enthusiastically searched for
an empty walnut shell to transport it in.

Yet, watching the blackbird devour
the latest batch of dried blackberries,
Snowdrop's heart sank. Even if she had
access to an endless store of fruit and nuts,
it seemed impossible to feed this nesting
mother fast enough. She knew that what her
friend really needed was a juicy worm or
some grubs, and catching insects was strictly
against the Flower Fairy Law. Snowdrop
gulped. If only she knew where the male bird
had gone . . . Not wanting to seem glum, she
forced a cheery smile and continued to wrack
her brains as to what she could usefully do.

The blackbird wiped her beak on her
feathers, and focused on the petite Garden

Fairy, her dark eyes full of gratitude. "My dear," she chirruped, "you have been more than kind, and I can see that you're exhausted ..."

"Oh, it's nothing," Snowdrop said, blushing modestly.

"No. You've saved me—there's no question of that. But there's one more favor—" She

paused for a moment
and then solemnly asked,
"Would you be so good
as to sit on the nest for an
hour?" The request was still
hanging in the air as the blackbird
continued, "While you've been away, I've
managed to pull out some of my downy
feathers. We could spread them over the
eggs . . . and I wouldn't be gone for long.
It's just that I'm worried about my mate.
He's been away for a whole day and a night
. . . So, while I've got the energy, if it's not too
much trouble, I'd like to go . . ."

Snowdrop knew it was rude to interrupt,
but she didn't need to be asked twice. She'd
already promised that everything would
be all right and this was something that
she could actually do to help. "I'll do it. I'll
do it!" she gushed. Then, trying to look as

dependable as possible, she pulled herself
upright and said firmly, "It would be an
honor to look after your eggs. Now—go!
And don't you worry about a thing."

Chapter Three

Glorious Snow!

"Anyone for more tea?" Winter Jasmine asked merrily.

Egg-sitting had turned into a social event. Soon after the blackbird had departed, Winter Jasmine had come across Snowdrop sitting cross-legged atop the nest, taking her responsibility very seriously. Then, when Box Tree had gone to fetch a pile of moss blankets from the tree trunk, he'd bumped into Hazel-Catkin, who'd been curious to take a look too.

Now, the four Flower Fairies were munching on seed cake and sipping hot chamomile tea,

expecting the blackbird and her mate to return at any moment.

"It's never made sense to me that they're called *black*birds," Hazel-Catkin mused, resting her chin on her knees. "I mean, the females would be better off being called *brown*birds, wouldn't they?"

Snowdrop giggled. It was true. The male bird with his shiny black plumage was well-named, whereas the female had soft brown feathers that were speckled in places. She wondered where her friend had got to and

hoped that she'd had a good feast before flying off in search of her mate. Ever so gently, she reached down and lifted a feather to touch the smooth shell of one of the eggs. It felt nice and warm. Soon its parents would be back, her job would be done and everything would be all right, just as she'd promised . . .

"Snowdrop—wake up!"
"Mmmm?" Snowdrop felt groggy and disorientated. It was pitch-black and she

couldn't see anything. Where was she?

"It's the middle of the night and the blackbirds still aren't back," said a voice that she recognized as Winter Jasmine's.

All at once, it came flooding back. At sunset, there had still been no sign of the birds and the assembled Flower Fairies had begun to get sleepy. Snowdrop was determined to stay awake for their arrival, but after the excitement of discovering the nest, and then the tiring task of delivering food, it had been a long day. She had been worried about damaging the eggs in her sleep, so Winter Jasmine, who had made a temporary bed next to the nest, suggested that they took it in turns to sit on the nest, and to sleep.

"I think it's time that we did something, Snowdrop," her friend said earnestly. "It's got really cold and I'm not sure that we'll be able to keep the eggs warm enough for much longer. And—er—what if they start to hatch?" Snowdrop suddenly felt awake. Wide awake. Winter Jasmine was right. The darkness had brought about a serious temperature drop which was a real risk to the unborn chicks. It was time to take some serious action—but what? The little Flower Fairy furrowed her brow and rubbed some life back into her arms while she thought. There was only one thing for it—they had to organize a large-scale search party and that would involve a lot of fairies.

Snowdrop jumped to her feet. She knew what they had to do. "We're going to need the help of Kingcup and Queen of the Meadow," she announced.

Hibernation was going to have to end early this year.

Once Snowdrop had set her mind on going to find the king and queen of Flower Fairyland, she'd given Winter Jasmine strict instructions to keep himself covered and not to move from the nest. It was a long way to the marsh and would be a difficult journey, particularly at night. But there was no time to lose and she didn't have a better idea.

As Snowdrop crawled along, she felt icy fingers of cold air reaching towards her, chilling her to the bone. And she was surprised to see a dull white light rather than the inky blackness that she'd been expecting. She was planning to fly directly to Box Tree's

hedge to ask him to accompany her on her
mission, but when she stuck her head out of
the tunnel, she was frozen to the spot by the
glorious sight that met her eyes.

The garden—or what she could see of it—
was covered in a thick blanket of dazzling
white snow, and it was getting deeper by
the minute. The sky was a mass of huge
swirling flakes and as Snowdrop stared
up at them, they stuck to her face
and got caught in her eyelashes.

"Wow!" she exclaimed,
feeling a thrill of
excitement. It was
just beautiful.

She had only seen a big snowfall on a handful of occasions and never before at night. The garden was shrouded in a deep silence and a crisp carpet of undisturbed snow lay on the ground. She was completely mesmerized.

Then, suddenly, snapping out of her daze, Snowdrop remembered her mission. There must have been a blizzard in the last few hours to create such thick coverage, which would be the reason that the blackbirds hadn't returned to the nest. "They could be trapped," she worried out loud, opening her wings. If they were, she realized, she was wholly responsible for looking after their eggs. "Right. There's no time to lose," she said with determination, despite feeling a bit shaky about the task that lay ahead. Then she launched herself into mid-air and, in order to make progress through the falling snow, began beating her wings as hard as she could.

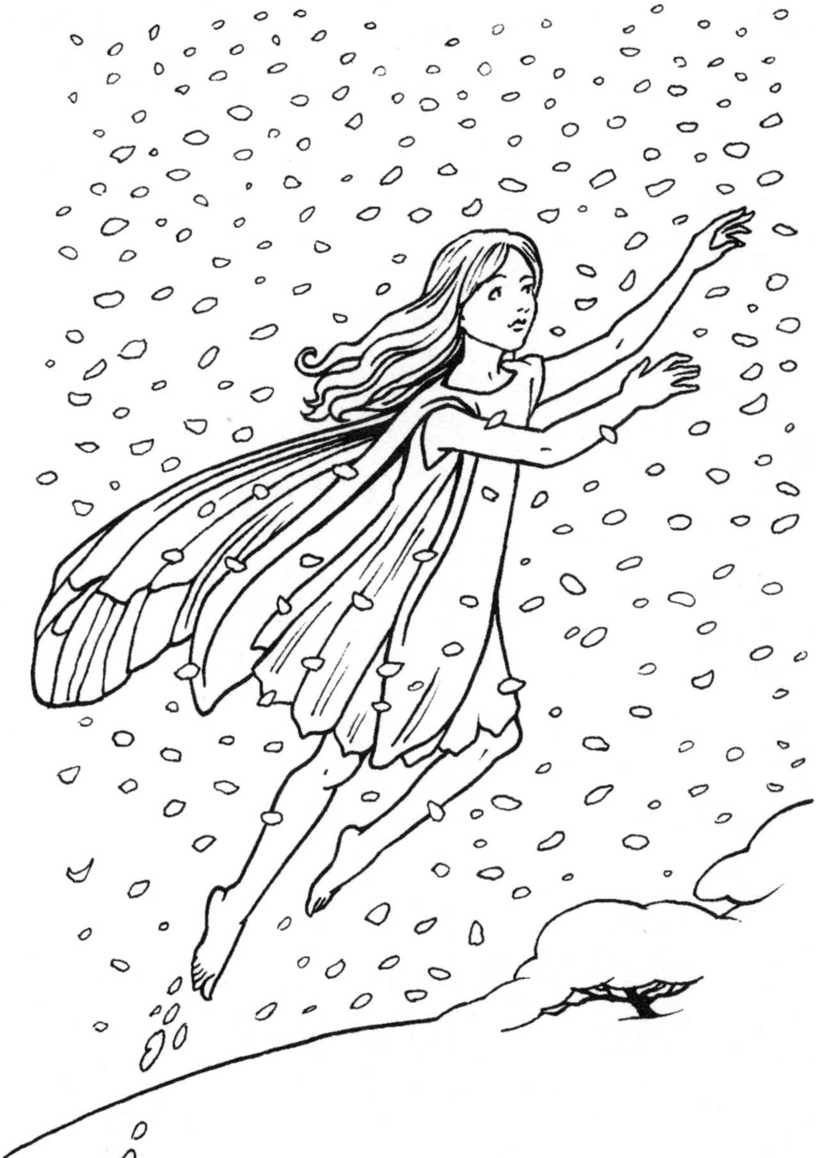

Tu-whit, tu-whoo.
Tu-whit, tu-whoo.
"Goodness!"
Snowdrop started at
the nearness of the
owl call.

"That's my friend
Tawny." Box Tree
grinned. Then his
eyes widened. "That's
it! Of course. I've got
it!"

Snowdrop had no idea what he was
referring to. The two of them had been trying
to figure out how to find the marsh without

losing their bearings in the snowstorm. And she had begun to feel anxious about Winter Jasmine trying to keep the eggs warm all on his own.

"The owl. He'll take you to Kingcup and Queen of the Meadow. He can see in the dark, and he's strong and fast." Box Tree nodded with enthusiasm. "And I'll take all the warm blankets and rugs that I've got— and some food—and go and give Winter Jasmine a hand."

"Oh, you're brilliant!" Snowdrop congratulated him.

Her friend shrugged modestly, then, losing no time, cupped his hands and made a strange call that echoed out into the still night. *Gu, gu-rooh. Gu, gu-rooh.*

Snowdrop was about to speak when Box Tree lifted a finger to his lips. "Listen," he whispered.

The two fairies waited in silence and, within just a few moments, there was a call of recognition from the owl. *Gu, gu-rooh. Gu, gu-rooh.*

"He's coming." Box Tree beamed.

And, sure enough, out of the darkness appeared a huge owl swooping down towards them.

Although they were travelling at quite a speed, Snowdrop didn't feel the cold air whistling past. She was lying on her tummy in the deep tawny feathers of the owl's back, with her arms wrapped firmly round his neck and her feet burrowed underneath her for warmth. At first she had felt nervous of the large bird with his dark, deep-set eyes, hooked beak and sharp talons. But when he exchanged a series of friendly hoots with Box Tree and then dipped his head in agreement at their request, her fear subsided. Indeed, he had stayed very still and been ever so gentle when she'd climbed up on his back. And he'd told her to call him Tawny, like Box did, and assured her that they would reach their destination in no time.

The owl's strong wings flapped noiselessly and effortlessly and, as promised, it seemed as though they had barely left the ground before he was already making his descent down towards the marsh.

"Th-thank you," Snowdrop said, as they landed. "Brrrrrr." She couldn't help shivering at the prospect of climbing off his back and searching for the king and queen of Flower Fairyland.

"I'm not going to drop you in a snow drift and expect you to find your own way!" Tawny hooted. He seemed to have read her mind.

"Oh, you've done more than enough," the Garden Fairy replied, trying to sound brave.

"Nonsense," the owl retorted over his shoulder. "Kingcup is a personal friend of mine—I often take him on tours of the kingdom—so I know just where to find him. And, no disrespect, but your little wings will never get you back to the garden in this weather."

Although they hadn't been acquainted for long, she couldn't help giving him an affectionate squeeze. She was incredibly grateful. Snowdrop didn't know the marsh at

all and although it had stopped snowing and her eyes had grown accustomed to the dark, all she could see was a huge expanse of snow-covered land, dotted with pools of frozen water. There was no plant life to give her any clue of where to start looking for Kingcup or Queen of the Meadow and time was ticking away. *Every single minute could be crucial to the eggs' survival*, she thought. It was time to set her plan in motion.

It was completely unnatural to be woken midway through hibernation and Snowdrop felt guilty about it. She was also worried that Kingcup and Queen of the Meadow might be cross with her for disturbing their sleep or, at the very least, too disorientated to help.

Tawny had taken her to an old rabbit burrow, which he'd informed her was used by some of the wild marsh fairies during the winter months. He pulled out the wad of matted cotton-grass that blocked the entrance and then crouched low to the ground so that she could slide off his back.

"I'll wait for you here," he'd told her. "Good luck!"

Snowdrop had never ventured through a rabbit's hole before and was surprised to find that the walls and ground were almost completely smooth. As the earth was frozen, it was hard-going keeping her balance and it wasn't long before she'd slipped on to her bottom and begun

sliding down the slope, picking up speed as she went.

"Aaaaaggggghhhh!" she squealed, hurtling round a final corner. The little Garden Fairy burst into the main chamber of the burrow and before she could stop herself, had landed on a moss bed, right next to a sleeping Flower Fairy!

It was Queen of the Meadow. "What? What is it?" The royal fairy sat up as if a bolt of lightning had hit her. However, despite having been deeply asleep, her fluffy blonde hair was still set in a perfect golden halo and she didn't look the least bit rumpled. Climbing out of her cocoon of fluffy blankets, she stretched and smiled serenely. It made her look more approachable and it gave Snowdrop the courage that she needed to speak up.

"I'm so sorry to disturb you," she said, picking herself up to give the queen a bit of space, "but I need your help, and . . . and . . . it's an emergency!"

"Now, calm down and start from the beginning." Queen of the Meadow reached out and patted Snowdrop's arm. "Whatever it is, we can definitely sort it out."

While they had been talking, fairies from the adjoining chambers had begun to stir and, as Snowdrop told her story, first Cotton-Grass, followed by Mallow, then Rush-Grass and finally, Kingcup himself, gathered round and listened to what she had to say.

When the Garden Fairy had finished talking, she looked to Queen of the Meadow for a response, but it was Kingcup who spoke

first.

"You have been very brave," the handsome fairy said, "and you were quite right to wake us. You made a promise to the blackbird—and a Flower Fairy promise is not to be taken lightly." The king's kind words brought tears to Snowdrop's eyes; she couldn't have wished for a better response. He continued, "Now, we'll get organized, and I give you my solemn vow that the blackbirds will be found and reunited with their eggs by morning."

Chapter Five
A New Dawn

All the Garden Fairies could do now, was wait. And hope.

Kingcup had promised Snowdrop that he would personally lead a search party to locate the missing blackbirds and, in turn, Queen of the Meadow had suggested enlisting the help of the field mice, who were really fast runners and could cover a large area quickly. Then they'd sent Snowdrop back to the garden with Tawny and reassured her that they'd keep her informed of any progress.

Once she'd thanked the owl at least five times and they'd exchanged goodbyes, Snowdrop had crawled as quickly as she could into the depths of the winter jasmine bush, eager to find out how the nest-sitters had fared. The sight of the two boys sitting cross-legged on top of the pile of moss blankets that they'd carefully spread out over the eggs, brought a smile to her lips. They almost looked like mother hens!

"Snowdrop!" yelled Box Tree happily, catching sight of her. "How did it go?"

"Better than I could have dared hope," Snowdrop replied. And she went on to tell them all about her comfortable flight and how wonderful the wild fairies had been. They made her describe her less-than-graceful entrance more than once and both roared with laughter at the thought of her skidding to a halt virtually on top of the

Queen herself!

"And you've done a great job, too," Snowdrop praised them, once they'd stopped laughing.

Winter Jasmine's expression of glee disappeared instantly. "The eggs seem to be fine—for now, but it's the very early part of the morning that's the coldest," he said seriously.

"You're right," Snowdrop replied. "I hadn't thought of that. I had it in my mind that the blackbirds would be back soon and that all our worries would be over."

Winter Jasmine shook his head. "I know that Kingcup will do everything in his power to find them, but. . ." he broke off, obviously not wanting to voice his thoughts, "what happens if something dreadful has happened and they don't come back?"

"Oh, don't," Box wimpered. "We've got to stay positive. There must be something that we can do."

"Absolutely," said Snowdrop, trying to sound confident. They'd come too far to fall at the final hurdle. She crouched down close to the eggs and closed her eyes to concentrate. "We need a miracle," she murmured.

No sooner had the words left her lips then her eyes flew open and she was on her feet. "Of course! We can't perform miracles, but each of us is capable of a little bit of magic!"

"You mean fairy dust!" Winter Jasmine exclaimed.

"Exactly," Snowdrop replied, reaching into the pocket of her dress and producing a small packet. It was a folded sycamore leaf and inside it were tiny particles of ground-up pollen. Each of the Flower Fairies made fairy dust from their own special plant and it was just powerful enough to give a helping hand in times of need. "Stand back a minute," she commanded. "I need it to fall directly on the eggs."

Immediately, the boys climbed down

from their perch and carefully began to peel back the layers of moss and feathers. Acting quickly, so as not to lose any precious heat, Snowdrop took a large pinch of the magic powder and sprinkled it liberally over the blue-grey eggs. As it fell, landing in a fine layer on their shells, she chanted a spell:

"Fairy dust, fairy dust—make the eggs

warm. Keep them cosy from now until dawn."

The three friends held their breath and waited to see what would happen. Sure enough, within seconds, the particles of dust began to shimmer, and putting a hand just above one egg's surface, Snowdrop announced, "It's working—there's a warm glow coming off them!"

"Well done!" said Box. "And when your dust loses its power, I've got some to keep the spell going."

"Me too," added Winter Jasmine.

"You know," said Snowdrop, "If we work as a team and make sure the glow doesn't go out— we might just make it!"

* * *

Tap tap tap.

Snowdrop's eyes snapped open. She wasn't asleep, but she had fallen into a trance and her eyelids had become heavy. The Garden Fairies had decided to take it in turns to watch the eggs and sprinkle more fairy dust on them whenever the magic began to wear off. Each one of them was exhausted from their busy night and immediately fell into a deep sleep the moment they came off duty.

Tap tap tap.

There it was again. But what was making that noise? Snowdrop looked around.

Tap tap tap.

It sounded as though it was coming from the eggs. *Surely not.*

Snowdrop shook her head and blinked several times in an attempt to come to her senses. She leaned over the side of the twiggy nest to take a closer look.

"Oh no! Oh goodness!" she yelped as she located the source of the tapping.

One of the four eggs had a crack in it—and it was rapidly turning into a small hole. It was hatching!

Her cries had woken the boys and it didn't take them more than a few seconds to understand the cause of her distress.

"What are we going to do?" Box Tree's eyes were like saucers.

"Um—not panic?" suggested Winter Jasmine, sounding less than convinced.

"Look!" said Snowdrop. She was pointing at the egg. "Oh, look!"

For there, just visible, was a tiny yellow beak, pecking away at the inside of the shell. And, at that moment, more tap-tapping started up and a crack appeared in a second, then a third, egg. The baby chicks were well and truly on their way—and there was nothing the Flower Fairies could do to stop them!

Chapter Six
A Surprise for Snowdrop

Snowdrop's mind was in a whirl. *So* much had happened.

While the three friends were still marvelling at the miracle of the baby chicks, Rush-Grass had come bursting into their midst with the good news that the blackbirds had been found and were on their way.

He told them that the male's wing had

been injured by a falling branch when he was foraging for food on the forest floor. Unable to fly, he'd hidden himself in a holly bush, hoping to regain his strength sufficiently to make the long journey back to the nest. By the time his mate found him, his wing was much better but then the blizzard started and they both knew that flying in treacherous conditions would be foolish. So they'd remained sheltered in the bush, worrying terribly that it would be impossible for Snowdrop to keep their eggs warm overnight.

"Anyway, we took Self-Heal with us," Rush-Grass explained. "And she said she'd make his wing as good as new in no time." The Wild Fairy paused for breath—he'd been gabbling away. "That's when I left—but they should be here any moment—they can fly much faster than me, of course."

While he had been talking, the final egg had cracked and now there were four skinny pink fledglings, tweeting non-stop for food, but with their eyes still shut tight. They were *so* sweet. All at once, Snowdrop felt overwhelmed with relief. She grinned at her two friends. She just couldn't believe that they had made it through the night and now

a new day was dawning. But then she realized that she hadn't said anything yet to Rush-Grass—there had been just too much to take in all at once.

"That's wonderful," she croaked. She took the wild fairy's hand in hers, "Thank you.

Thank you so much."

Usually, as soon as Snowdrop's flowers arrived, she would move back outside, but the snow was still thick on the ground and it was freezing. In fact, her plants were virtually buried and the bowed white flower heads were only really visible if you knew where to look. Once she'd left the winter jasmine bush, she'd gone to check on them, feeling she'd been a bit neglectful in the last day or so. They were fine, of course. Contrary to their delicate appearance, they were incredibly tough and used to the cold.

Once the Garden Fairies had witnessed the blackbirds' happy reunion with their young, they'd excused themselves—so that the parents could get on with the task of feeding them without distraction. The female blackbird had made them promise that once

they'd rested, they'd come back and visit—
she wanted to hear all about the nest-sitters'
adventure, and thank them properly.

Despite having slept for most of the day,
Snowdrop felt as if she'd barely laid her head
down when Hazel-Catkin had called by to
let her know that Kingcup and Queen of the
Meadow were holding a meeting. " We're to
go back to the winter jasmine bush!" she'd
called over her shoulder before rushing off
to smarten up her appearance. Now she had
returned.

"Snowdrop—it's me, Hazel-Catkin. Are
you ready?" The Tree Fairy stuck her head
into the hollow trunk.

"As ready as I'll ever be," Snowdrop
replied nervously. Reluctantly, she pulled a
comb through her tangled hair and changed
into a clean, uncreased dress. She knew she
looked presentable, but her stomach was full

of butterflies.

"Whatever do you mean?" asked her
friend, swinging her chestnut hair, which she
appeared to have brushed to a shine.

"Er, Kingcup, and Queen of the

Meadow—they're bound to want to tell me off for waking them up. And in front of everyone else too!" blurted out Snowdrop, tears welling in her eyes.

"Well, you could be right," Hazel-Catkin replied, sounding all mysterious. "But let's just wait and see." Smiling warmly, she grabbed Snowdrop's hand. "Come on, or we'll be late!"

It was the most magical sight she had ever seen.

As they rounded the corner, Snowdrop dragged her feet. All she expected to see was the familiar yellow blaze of the winter jasmine bush. But when she looked up, she couldn't believe her eyes. It was as if Hazel-Catkin had transported her to somewhere entirely different!

Leading up to the bush, nestled in the

snow, were Lords-and-Ladies' candles blinking in the dusk light. And tucked between the winter jasmine branches were festive sprigs of mistletoe and holly, with colorful petal parcels hanging off them. *What was going on?*

The air was heavy with a wonderful aroma, quite unlike anything Snowdrop had smelled before. As she took in the extraordinary scene, she noticed a huge platter piled high

with sticky-looking cakes and next to it
a steaming pot of *something* with a ladle
sticking out of it. "Orange and cinnamon
buns," Hazel-Catkin whispered, seeing her
friend wrinkle her nose quizzically, "and
Christmas punch."

"Christmas . . . what?" said Snowdrop,
suddenly wondering where everyone was.

"SURPRISE!"

At that moment a whole host of Flower
Fairies jumped out of the bush—Winter
Jasmine himself, followed by Box, Holly,
Mistletoe and Yew, and all the wild marsh

fairies including the king and queen.

"Welcome to your very own Christmas party," announced Kingcup, waving his arm regally. As always, he was resplendent, clothed almost entirely in shimmering gold, and on his arm was Queen of the Meadow—looking as pristine and elegant as ever.

"We thought you deserved a treat for all your hard work and clever thinking," said Winter Jasmine, winking at her.

"And you've always wanted to know what Christmas is like," added Box, holding out a cup of mouth-watering punch.

Just then the male blackbird popped his head out of the bush. "The chicks and my mate are resting," he chirruped. "So I've just come to give you our present—to say thank you. For *everything*."

Snowdrop, still lost for words, bobbed her head in reply. Then the jet-black bird, whose appearance was quite striking against the white ground, opened his orange beak and warbled the most beautiful song she had ever heard. It was all about the winter and how harsh it could be, but how Mother Nature never forgot to deliver symbols of hope.

When he had finished, all the Flower Fairies clapped and cheered—not least of all Snowdrop, and then he hopped back into the bush to join his family.

"Ahem," said Snowdrop, finally finding her voice. "I just wanted to say—to many of you here—that I'm sorry that I woke you up! But I'm really hoping that I'm forgiven now—as keeping a Flower Fairy promise and seeing the blackbirds reunited was definitely worth it." She paused and glanced at her friends gathered around her—all dressed up and ready to celebrate. Then, wiping away a tear of happiness that had run down her cheek, she continued. "And thank you—thank you for all of this. If I'm never awake for a proper Christmas, I will always remember my own very special winter wonderland!"

FLOWER FAIRIES™ FRIENDS

Visit our Flower Fairies website at:

www.flowerfairies.com

There are lots of fun Flower Fairy games and
activities for you to play, plus you can find out more
about all your favorite fairy friends!

Log onto the
Flower Fairies
Friendship Ring

Visit the Flower Fairies website to sign up for the new
Flower Fairies Friendship Ring!

★ No membership fee
★ News and updates
★ Every new friend receives a special gift!
(while supplies last)